The Ca~~se of~~

Mr. Colp looked baffled and angry.

"The spies are laughing at us," he said. "They know they're being watched. Yet somehow they're passing information under our noses. Otherwise, their living in the same hotel doesn't make sense."

Chief Brown gestured for Encyclopedia to slip out and investigate the bathroom.

The bathroom door stood open. Encyclopedia went in and closed the door behind him.

The room had a window, a toilet, a sink, and a shower. Encyclopedia searched every inch of everything.

He spent a moment staring at the mirror above the sink. Then he closed his eyes and thought his hardest.

"Of course," he murmured, and returned to room 303. . . .

Encyclopedia Brown and the Case of the Two Spies

DONALD J. SOBOL

Illustrated by Eric Velasquez

The Martin Inn

A SKYLARK BOOK
NEW YORK • TORONTO • LONDON • SYDNEY • AUCKLAND

For My Grandson
Gregory Morgan Sobol

RL3.0, 008–012

ENCYCLOPEDIA BROWN AND THE CASE OF THE TWO SPIES
A Syklark Book / published by arrangement with
Delacorte Press

PRINTING HISTORY
Delacorte Press edition published March 1994
Skylark edition published April 1995

ISBN 0-553-48297-1

Published simultaneously in the United States and Canada

Bantam Books are published by Bantam Books, a division of Bantam
Doubleday Dell Publishing Group, Inc. Its trademark, consisting of
the words "Bantam Books" and the portrayal of a rooster, is Registered
in U.S. Patent and Trademark Office and in other countries. Marca
Registrada. Bantam Books, 1540 Broadway, New York, New York 10036.

PRINTED IN THE UNITED STATES OF AMERICA

CWO   0 9 8 7

Contents

The Case of the Kidnapped Dog

Idaville looked like an ordinary seaside town.

It had beautiful beaches, four banks, and two delicatessens. It had churches, a synagogue, and a Little League.

Still, there was something mysterious about Idaville.

For more than a year no one, grown-up or child, had gotten away with breaking the law there.

Policemen from coast to coast wondered, how did Idaville do it?

Only three people knew the answer, and they weren't telling.

The three lived in a red brick house at 13 Rover Avenue—Mr. Brown, Mrs. Brown, and their only child, ten-year-old Encyclopedia, America's crime-buster in sneakers.

Mr. Brown was chief of police. He was honest, brave,

and wise. Especially wise. Whenever he had a puzzling case, he did what was necessary. He went home.

Encyclopedia solved the case for him at the dinner table. Usually before dessert. Usually with one question.

Chief Brown would have liked Encyclopedia's sneakers bronzed and hung in the Smithsonian Institution in Washington, D.C.

But he knew that could never be. Who would take him seriously? Who would believe that the mastermind behind Idaville's war on crime was a fifth-grader?

So Chief Brown never boasted of his son. Neither did Mrs. Brown.

For his part Encyclopedia kept the secret. He never dropped a hint about the help he gave his father. Bragging was for people who didn't know enough.

But there was nothing he could do about his nickname.

Only his parents and his teachers called him by his real name, Leroy. Everyone else in Idaville called him Encyclopedia.

An encyclopedia is a book or set of books filled with facts from A to Z. So was Encyclopedia's head. He read more books than anybody, and he never forgot a word.

His pals said he was better than a computer for getting answers. His brain didn't stop during a power failure.

After saying grace Friday evening, Chief Brown stared at his cream of potato soup.

"I know that look, dear," Mrs. Brown said. "A case is troubling you. Give Leroy the facts. He hasn't failed you yet."

Chief Brown nodded. "I'm going to."

Encyclopedia instantly put down his spoon and came alert.

Chief Brown said, "Last Monday Mrs. Joan Todd's Great Dane was kidnapped."

"Royal Blackie?" exclaimed Mrs. Brown. "Oh, my! The dog is a champion!"

"Mrs. Todd received a ransom note in the mail yesterday," Chief Brown said.

He took a sheet of paper from his pocket and handed it to Mrs. Brown. "This is a copy of the ransom note."

"How strangely it's worded," murmured Mrs. Brown, who had taught English and other subjects in high school. She passed the sheet to Encyclopedia.

He read: *Mrs. Joan T.: Your pooch is okay. You may obtain him for $500. I shall inform you by horn on fifth of this month of a spot at which you must put your $500.*

"The fifth of the month is Sunday, two days from now," Chief Brown said. "That doesn't give us time to find the kidnapper."

"Why not?" Mrs. Brown asked. "You can catch him when he picks up the ransom money on Sunday."

"That may be true," Chief Brown answered. "However, Mrs. Todd can't wait until Sunday. The Idaville Kennel Club dog show is this Saturday. Royal Blackie has a good chance of winning Best in Class again—if he's there."

"Then you'll have to find Royal Blackie by tomorrow," Mrs. Brown said glumly.

A silence fell upon the room. Both parents stared at Encyclopedia. He hadn't said a word. He was not yet ready to ask his one question.

Chief Brown continued with the facts of the case.

"The ransom note was mailed three days ago in Idaville, according to the postmark. Chances are that someone living here is the kidnapper."

"What about the typewriter used to write it?" Mrs. Brown said. "No two typewriters print the same. They're like fingerprints, aren't they?"

"Yes," Chief Brown agreed. "However, this note was written on a computer and printed on a laser printer made by the Mayfair Company. Laser printers print alike."

"Then you don't have a clue?" Mrs. Brown said.

"I have a lead," Chief Brown said. "Last month two Idaville men bought Mayfair laser printers. I had the stores in town that sell computers check their records. The two men, Howard Bass and Hal Gibson, live near Mrs. Todd. Both have complained to the police about Royal Blackie getting into their vegetable gardens last month."

"So the dog wasn't kidnapped for the ransom money?" Mrs. Brown said.

"Hardly likely, or the kidnapper would have asked for more than five hundred dollars," Chief Brown said. "He probably wants revenge for what Royal Blackie did to his vegetable garden. What better way than to make the dog miss the dog show!"

Chief Brown paused. Then he said, "That's about it."

He regarded Encyclopedia hopefully. So did Mrs. Brown.

The boy detective had closed his eyes. He always closed his eyes when doing his deepest thinking.

After a few seconds he opened his eyes and asked his one question.

"Did Mr. Bass and Mr. Gibson go to college?"

Chief Brown seemed amazed by the question. "Y-yes," he answered. "Mr. Bass is a lawyer. Mr. Gibson is an engineer. What has their education to do with the kidnapping?"

"The ransom note doesn't appear to be written by a college graduate," Encyclopedia observed.

Chief Brown frowned. "Then you don't think the kidnapper is Mr. Bass or Mr. Gibson?"

"I don't mean that, Dad," Encyclopedia declared.

"Perhaps Mr. Bass or Mr. Gibson tried to throw off suspicion by wording the ransom note poorly, like an uneducated man," Mrs. Brown said.

"No, or he would have purposefully misspelled a word or two," Encyclopedia answered.

"Well, what *do* you mean?" Chief Brown demanded.

"For one thing," Encyclopedia said, "the kidnapper wrote that he would inform Mrs. Todd where to leave the money 'on fifth of this month.' That's Sunday. Why didn't he write 'Sunday'?"

"I give up, Leroy," Chief Brown said. "Why?"

"Because he couldn't," Encyclopedia answered.

Chief Brown and Mrs. Brown seemed about to jump out of their seats.

"Leroy!" cried Chief Brown.

"Leroy!" cried Mrs. Brown.

"Who is the kidnapper?" they cried together.

Encyclopedia smiled. "He has to be—"

Who Is Royal Blackie's Kidnapper?

(Turn to page 64 for the solution to
The Case of the Kidnapped Dog.)

The Case of the Fireflies

Encyclopedia helped his father solve mysteries through-
out the year. During the summer he helped children in the
neighborhood as well.

When school let out, he opened his own detective
agency in the family garage. Every morning he hung out
his sign:

Brown Detective Agency
13 Rover Avenue
LEROY BROWN
President
No case too small
25¢ a day plus expenses

The last customer Thursday afternoon was Fanchon
DuBois.

Fanchon was born in France and was into flies. She was known on the block as French Fannie the Female Fly Catcher.

"Bugs Meany stole my fireflies," she blurted.

"Oh, boy." Encyclopedia groaned. "Bugs never quits."

Bugs Meany was the leader of a gang of tough older boys. They called themselves the Tigers. In Encyclopedia's opinion they should have called themselves the Shoelaces. When they weren't tied up cheating little kids, they were at loose ends.

"Tell me what happened," Encyclopedia said.

"Ten minutes ago I was running down Brickell Avenue with a can of fireflies," Fanchon said. "Bugs Meany stopped me. He asked, 'What's the big hurry?' I told him I had three minutes to mail off my fireflies before the post office closed."

"Why were you mailing them?" Encyclopedia asked.

"A company in Texas has some seven hundred kids in twenty states catching fireflies," Fanchon said. "The company gives us nets and a special storage can that kills and dries the fireflies. We get a penny for each one."

"So Bugs just up and grabbed the can from you?"

"Not right away," Fanchon answered. "First he laughed and said little girls shouldn't play with fireflies. That burned me good. I lost my temper."

"Go on," Encyclopedia said.

"Like a dope I told him the fireflies were worth a penny apiece," Fanchon said. "That's when he grabbed the can."

She laid a quarter on the gas can beside Encyclopedia.

"I want to hire you to get back my fireflies. Bugs must

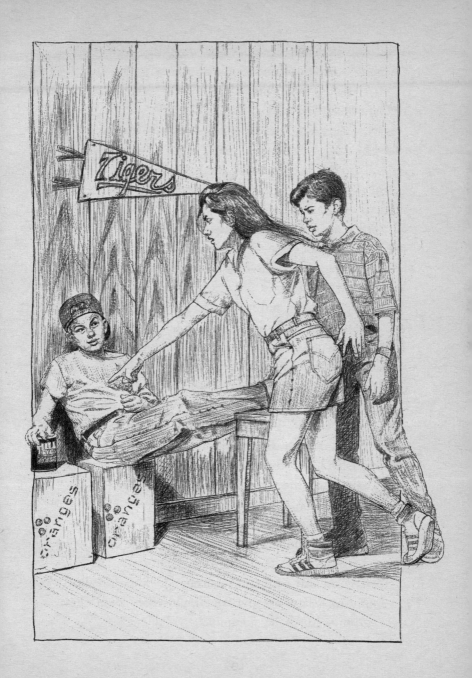

still have them. He wouldn't have had time to mail them off before the post office closed."

"I'll go see him," Encyclopedia said. "But you'll have to come along."

"Not me," Fanchon protested. "I don't want to get rid of my health."

"You have to come with me," Encyclopedia insisted. "Otherwise I won't know your can if I see it. Don't be afraid. I've handled Bugs before."

"All right," Fanchon muttered uneasily. "But I could use something for the headache I'm about to have."

The Tigers' clubhouse was an empty toolshed behind Mr. Sweeney's auto body shop. On the way to it Fanchon and Encyclopedia talked fireflies.

"The male lights up to let the female know he's around," Encyclopedia recalled. "The female waits in bushes or in tall grass and flashes her light to show she's interested."

"Right," Fanchon said.

"I read about the company that sends you the cans," Encyclopedia said. "When the cans are full, you mail them back. The part of the firefly that lights up is sold to hospitals and laboratories for medical purposes."

"Good golly, Encyclopedia!" Fanchon gasped. "Is there anything you don't know?"

A minute later they reached the Tigers' clubhouse. Bugs Meany was alone. Beside him on an orange crate was a can.

"That's my can," Fanchon murmured. "I'm sure of it."

Bugs saw them and snarled, "Look what's come down the beanstalk. Make like a bumblebee and buzz off."

"I wish he wouldn't talk like that," Fanchon whispered.

"Fanchon says you stole her can of fireflies, Bugs," Encyclopedia said calmly.

"Fan her head!" Bugs roared. "This kid's been sniffing too many gumdrops." He advanced on Fanchon, teeth bared.

Fanchon turned pale and she took off. Encyclopedia was left to face the Tigers' leader alone.

"That's her can on the orange crate," he said.

Bugs sneered. "You must have a leak in your think tank. Me and my Tigers caught those fireflies."

Therewith he closed his eyes, raised his eyebrows, and gently sniffed the breeze.

"Everybody takes me for an unfeeling roughneck." He sighed. "Fact is, me and my Tigers are nature lovers at heart."

"Next you're going to tell me you caught those fireflies in the stadium last night," Encyclopedia said.

The stadium was in South Park. It was completely enclosed by a wooden fence, but the gates were never locked.

Bugs smirked. "Good try, wise guy. It was raining last night. We caught the fireflies there Tuesday night after the girls' softball doubleheader."

"Since when have you been interested in fireflies?"

"Us Tigers are working to save energy," Bugs declared. "We're going to turn fireflies into cheap light and earn the thanks of a grateful nation."

"The fireflies in the can couldn't light up a buttonhole," Encyclopedia pointed out. "They're dead."

Bugs received the news like a camel with the staggers. He recovered quickly, however.

"Those fireflies aren't for light," he said. "They're for research. We're studying them. We have to move carefully, step by step, like all true scientists. Thomas Edison didn't invent the lightbulb in a day, you know."

"Give it up, Bugs," Encyclopedia said. "The fireflies belong to Fanchon. You didn't catch them."

What Was Bugs's Mistake?

**(Turn to page 65 for the solution to
The Case of the Fireflies.)**

The Case of
the Duck Derby

Bugs Meany hated being outsmarted by Encyclopedia Brown all the time. He longed to get even.

Bugs never used his muscles, however. Whenever he felt like it, he remembered Sally Kimball. Sally was Encyclopedia's junior partner in the detective agency.

She was also the prettiest girl in the fifth grade. And she could do what no little kid thought was possible.

Punch out Bugs Meany.

Whenever they traded blows, the toughest Tiger ended on his back, as full of fight as a ten-minute egg.

"Bugs doesn't like you any better than he does me," Encyclopedia warned Sally. "His brain is working overtime at revenge."

"We're safe," Sally said. "If you planted Bugs's brain in a goldfish, it would drown."

The two detectives were biking to South Park for the yearly Duck Derby. People from all over the state had flocked there to watch the ducks run.

The detectives parked their bikes under a banyan tree. Encyclopedia saw Cecy Wenor, a classmate, approaching through the crowd. She was carrying a duck.

"Isn't this great!" she exclaimed. "Two hundred ducks are entered in the races this year."

She held up her duck. "Meet Duck Amuck. . . . Hey, didn't you bring a racer?"

"No, we came to watch," Sally said.

"You're not too late for a chance to be in the winner's circle," Cecy said.

She led the detectives to a covered pen filled with ducks. A sign by the gate read:

RENT A DUCK FOR $5.00, PLUS $10 ENTRANCE FEE.

Cecy looked over the ducks and shook her head.

"Forget it," she said.

"What's wrong?" Sally asked.

"None of those waddlers can win," Cecy answered. "They're too old. Most ducks are fastest at four months, like Duck Amuck."

Cecy stroked Duck Amuck's feathers lovingly. "He's what I've been looking for all year," she said. "A small bird with long legs. He was born to race. You should see him do wind sprints."

The call for the start of the junior division races boomed over a loudspeaker.

"Here we go," Cecy said.

"Good luck," Encyclopedia said.

"Thanks, we'll need it," Cecy said. "There are lots of serious trainers here today. The winner of each heat gets a twenty-five-dollar savings bond. Top duck in the junior division gets a hundred-dollar bond."

"That's not exactly chicken feed," Encyclopedia murmured.

The detectives walked with Cecy to the racecourse. Eight lanes, fifteen feet long, were separated by wire fencing.

"Trainers can run along the ramp and shout encouragement to their ducks," Cecy explained. "But they can't touch them once the race has begun."

A judge announced the racers for the first heat. Eight web-footed sprinters, including Duck Amuck, were brought to the starting line.

The ducks took off at the starter's whistle.

Duck Amuck won by a beak over a fast fowl named Salty Quackers. The time was a swift 1.9 seconds.

The detectives watched five more heats. Before the sixth Encyclopedia saw Bugs Meany and Officer Muldoon closing in on him.

"There's the little thief!" Bugs cried, waving at Encyclopedia. "Arrest him in the name of the law!"

"Better come with me," the policeman said quietly.

Encyclopedia did as he was told. Sally followed him. People were staring.

"That no-good Bugs," Sally whispered. "He's pulling another of his dirty tricks."

The detectives followed Bugs and Officer Muldoon to the banyan tree where they had parked their bikes.

"Bugs says the basket on your bike belongs to him," Officer Muldoon said. "He claims you stole it."

"That's not true," Encyclopedia protested.

"His name is on the outside of the basket," Officer Muldoon replied sternly.

"I saw it when these two biked into the park," Bugs said. He pointed to the park entrance on his right.

"How could you see your name from so far away?" Sally demanded.

Bugs grinned. "I mean I saw the basket when you two rode into the park." He correctly traced the detectives' path to the tree with a leftward sweep of his arm. "I didn't see my name until Mr. Goody-Goody here passed five feet in front of me. There it was on the basket."

Encyclopedia examined the basket. BUGS MEANY was inked on the right side in big red letters.

"If only it were not true." Bugs sighed. "The son of our beloved chief of police is a cheap crook. Oh, the pity of it!"

"This is a frame-up," Sally said to Officer Muldoon. "Bugs is trying to get Encyclopedia in trouble. He must have written his name on the basket while we were watching the races!"

Bugs tilted his head toward Sally and rolled his eyes. "I have this one failing," he confessed. "I'll never understand the workings of the criminal mind."

Sally stamped her foot. "Encyclopedia, don't let Bugs get away with this!"

"He won't," Encyclopedia said calmly. "He wrote his name on my basket, all right."

What Was the Proof?

(Turn to page 66 for the solution to The Case of the Duck Derby.)

The Case of
the Sand Castle

Encyclopedia and Sally biked to the beach early Saturday morning to view the sand sculptures.

The day before, children and grown-ups had dug, shaped, and patted sand from dawn until dusk. Along the high-tide line had risen a wonderland of castles, animals, streets, and ships.

By nightfall only the winners among the grown-ups had been chosen. The judging of the children's sculptures had to be put off until morning.

The detectives were eager to see what Pablo Pizzaro had made. Pablo was Idaville's greatest ten-year-old artist.

The children's sculptures stood separate from the grown-ups'. Encyclopedia saw two castles, one lion, and one pile of lumps.

Nearby, three of the young artists, Kevin Baines, Marty

Ginsberg, and Lance Wills lay side by side, sunning themselves. All wore bathing suits and sunglasses.

Pablo, the youngest young artist, sat by himself. He spied the detectives and drooped over to them.

"Sorry we couldn't come yesterday," Encyclopedia apologized.

Pablo was in no condition to accept anything but misery. "Somebody smashed my castle," he fairly sobbed.

He led the detectives to the pile of lumps.

Sally was furious. "Encyclopedia, do you think one of the others did this? Kevin, Marty, and Lance have a better chance of winning now!"

Encyclopedia did not answer. He was studying the mess of barefoot prints in the dry sand by Pablo's ruins.

Marty and Lance, he had already observed, were barefoot. Kevin wore sandals.

"Can the footprints tell us who smashed Pablo's castle?" Sally asked.

"No chance," Pablo said. "There must have been two hundred people around the sculptures yesterday."

Encyclopedia stepped to the ocean side of Pablo's castle. The smooth, damp sand there was without a footprint. The only mark was the fresh high-tide line. The line stopped inches short of the ruined castle.

Pablo moaned. "We'll never find out who did it."

"Can you fix up what's left?" Encyclopedia asked.

Pablo moaned again, harder. "How? The judging starts in fifteen minutes."

"Tessie!" Sally suddenly exclaimed. "I might have known she'd show up wherever Kevin is."

Encyclopedia turned. He saw Tessie Bottoms, looking a little like a walrus in a pink bathing suit, and her poodle, Cuddles.

"Cuddles should be on a leash," Encyclopedia said.

"So should Tessie," declared Sally.

Sally didn't like Tessie, a big, pushy eighth-grader who tried to boss around little kids.

"Look at her pose for Kevin, will you!" Sally said disgustedly. "She thinks she has an hourglass figure, and she's right. It takes an hour to figure it out."

Cuddles bounded playfully among the boys before sniffing at Kevin's sandals.

"That pooch must be trained to pay attention to Kevin," Pablo observed. "Tessie's been chasing him since seventh grade."

"Cuddles can't help her get a date," Sally said. "Even the tide wouldn't take her out."

"Maybe she wanted to help Kevin win," Pablo said thoughtfully. "She could have flattened my castle at one sitting."

"Or she let Cuddles run through it," Sally said.

"Cuddles is in the clear," Pablo stated. "There isn't a paw print near the castle."

Cuddles had quit sniffing at Kevin's sandals and was eagerly licking Lance's ankle.

"Question Kevin, Lance, and Marty," Sally urged.

Encyclopedia nodded and walked over to the boys. "Were any of you in the ocean this morning?" he asked.

"No," the three boys grunted together.

"Have you taken a shower since you left the beach yesterday?"

The three boys growled, "Yes."

Another question would bring a fast punch in the nose. Encyclopedia was glad to see a man and woman approaching.

"The judges," Pablo whimpered.

"Please stand by your artwork, boys," the woman requested.

"You, too, Pablo," Encyclopedia said. "Go on. Tell them the lumps represent Baldwin Castle after William the Conqueror destroyed it in the eleventh century."

"He must have used an atomic bomb," Pablo said.

"Well, say it's modern art," Sally offered. "Modern art doesn't have to make sense."

For a moment Pablo looked like a dead fish on a slab. Then he blinked feebly and threw back his shoulders. "Okay, I'll give it a try."

Neither William the Conqueror nor modern art helped him, however. He was awarded last place.

Lance took third, Marty took second, Kevin took first, and Tessie took Kevin.

Cooing congratulations, she swished her arms around his waist and squeezed.

Kevin's jaw dropped sideways and he squeaked like a boy with a rusty tonsil.

Sally stared helplessly at Encyclopedia. "If you just had more time…."

"To discover who smashed Pablo's castle?" Encyclopedia smiled. "It was—"

Who Smashed the Sand Castle?

(Turn to page 67 for the solution to
The Case of the Sand Castle.)

The Case of
the Telephone Call

"**I** have a surprise for you, Leroy," Mrs. Brown said after dinner. "Cousin Derek is coming for the weekend."

"Great!" exclaimed Encyclopedia. He always looked forward to seeing his cousin.

Derek was seventeen and lived in Atlanta, Georgia. He arrived in time for dinner Friday. He ate quietly, hardly saying a word.

After dessert he excused himself and went to his room.

"What do you think is troubling him, Mom?" Encyclopedia asked.

"He was fired from his summer job last week," Mrs. Brown answered. "It has upset him terribly. Aunt Helen felt he needed a change. So she sent him to us for a few days."

"Why was he fired?" Chief Brown asked.

"They say he caused his company to miss a big order," Mrs. Brown replied. "Derek claims it wasn't his fault."

"Derek wouldn't lie," Chief Brown declared.

"Perhaps you can speak with him, Leroy," Mrs. Brown said. "You might find out what really happened."

Encyclopedia agreed to try. He wasn't hopeful, though. Idaville was a long way from Atlanta, Georgia. Any clues would have to come from Derek's memory.

The detective went up to the guest room. Derek was lying on the bed, staring at the ceiling.

Encyclopedia began by asking about the Yankees, Derek's favorite baseball team. It was hard at first, but he finally got Derek talking.

When Encyclopedia saw his chance, he said, "Mom told me that you lost your summer job."

"I was fired," Derek corrected. "They said I left work early. I didn't. It's not losing the job that hurts so much. It's losing the chance to win a scholarship."

He explained. His job had been with a small shoe company in Atlanta. Every four years the shoe industry awarded a college scholarship to a high school student working at one of its member companies.

"You have to have good grades in school first," Derek said. "Then you have to be a good worker. Getting fired rules out my chance for the scholarship."

"Do you mind telling me what happened?" Encyclopedia asked.

Derek shrugged. "Last Monday Mr. Barton, the owner, left before noon. He had a headache. Mrs. Miller, his secretary, left at three-thirty. Her mother was in an automobile accident."

Derek sat up and took a deep breath.

"My job is in the stockroom," he went on. "But on days when both Mr. Barton and Mrs. Miller leave early, I go to the office and stay there till five o'clock. Then I can go home."

"What do you do in the office?"

"I answer the phone and take messages."

"How late did you stay in the office on Monday?"

"I left at five o'clock, when I'm supposed to," Derek answered. "Mr. Barton claims I left earlier. He says I missed an important telephone call at four-thirty."

"What made him think that?"

"When I leave, I turn on the answering machine on Mrs. Miller's desk. If the phone isn't answered after four rings, Mr. Barton's recorded voice comes on. It says, 'I cannot come to the phone now. At the sound of the beep, please leave the time, your name, message, and phone number. I'll get back to you when I can.'"

Derek slapped his thigh angrily.

"The phone didn't ring while I was in the office between three-thirty and five o'clock," he protested. "Mrs. Miller played back the answering machine the next morning. There was a message from a shoe company in California. She claimed the caller gave the time as four-thirty."

"Did Mr. Barton hear the recording?" Encyclopedia asked.

"No, just Mrs. Miller. She told Mr. Barton about it. I told him the phone never rang!"

"You didn't leave the office, even for a few minutes?" Encyclopedia asked.

"Absolutely not," Derek said. "I was in the office until five o'clock."

"What was the call on the answering machine about?"

"It was a rush order for five hundred of Mr. Barton's new two-way slippers," Derek replied. "You can put them on from either end."

"Wow!" Encyclopedia exclaimed. "That may be the greatest invention since cheesecake. Mr. Barton must be some kind of genius."

"Mr. Barton lives in his own world," Derek said. "He can't remember what month it is. But he's great at inventing. Last year he invented a sneaker with a ball in the arch. It makes you walk on your toes. You burn calories like crazy."

"Did Mr. Barton lose the order for the two-way slippers because no one got the call till the next morning?"

"And how," Derek answered. "The slippers had to be shipped the same day, or not at all. Mr. Barton threw a fit....Say, do you think Mrs. Miller lied about the time of the call in order to get me fired?"

"No," Encyclopedia said. "Everyone was just too upset to think straight. Mrs. Miller's mother was in an automobile accident. Mr. Barton lost a big order. You were fired. Cheer up. You'll get your job back."

What Made Encyclopedia So Sure?

**(Turn to page 68 for the solution to
The Case of the Telephone Call.)**

The Case of
the Stolen Wallet

One of Encyclopedia's good pals was Benny Breslin.

Everyone liked Benny—until he went to sleep. Then his nose was not only seen but heard.

When Benny slept on his side, his snoring didn't bother a soul. But when he slept on his back, it sounded as if walls were cracking and pipes were breaking up and down the block.

"If it's true that snoring grows worse with age, Benny will have to sleep in a bomb shelter someday," Charlie Stewart told Encyclopedia.

The two boys were getting ready for a weekend camping trip. Benny was joining them. His father had bought him a six-man tent. Benny was eager to use it.

"Benny's snoring kept us awake till midnight on our last camping trip," Charlie said. "We've got to find a way to keep him quiet tonight."

"It'd be easier to make an elephant tiptoe through wet cement," said Encyclopedia.

Charlie clicked his tongue thoughtfully. "Benny won't snore if we can keep him off his back and stop him from breathing through his mouth."

"We'd better just stuff our ears with cotton," Encyclopedia advised, "and go to sleep before Benny."

"Is that your best plan?" Charlie asked.

"Yes."

"What's your next best?"

"There isn't one."

"Well, let's hope for the best," Charlie said, wincing a little as he spoke.

The boys loaded their bikes and rode to the camping grounds west of South Park.

Benny was already there. With him were his two cousins, Todd and Garth.

Encyclopedia knew Todd and Garth. They were not what anyone would call quick thinkers.

Benny shouted a greeting and pointed proudly at his big new tent, which stood on the high ground behind him.

"It has everything," he exclaimed. "Flooring; chain-corded frames, double-needle lockstitched seams—"

"What about soundproofing?" Charlie mumbled under his breath.

Encyclopedia gave Charlie a hushing elbow. "The tent is great, Benny," he said.

The five boys laid out their places inside the tent. Charlie ended up beside Benny, with Todd on Benny's other side.

After hanging a garbage bag out of reach of raccoons, the

boys tossed a football and explored the woods. At five o'clock they headed for Mill Creek to do some fishing.

They chose a spot where the creek widened like a pond for a hundred yards. The water was silky.

"This time of year," Encyclopedia said, "the trout will be feeding near the surface."

The boys stood still, listening. The faint *slp*, *slp*, *slp* of trout feeding carried over the water.

For the next two hours the whine of lines being cast sliced the air. Encyclopedia and Charlie each caught a big trout. Benny caught three.

Benny gave all the credit to his lucky number 13 Detroit Lions shirt. He always wore the shirt when fishing. At night he changed into his other Lions shirt. It had the number 12 on the back. He loved the Lions.

"We have fish for everybody," Charlie said as night fell. "Time to head in."

Todd and Garth wanted to stay longer. They hadn't caught a keeper. They were overruled.

On the hike back to camp Encyclopedia whispered to Charlie, "Todd and Garth are really steamed at you. You made them throw back all their fish."

"They were too small," Charlie snapped angrily.

At the campsite Charlie built a fire while Todd and Garth glared at him. Benny cleaned the fish. Encyclopedia fried them.

The boys ate hungrily. Between mouthfuls they talked sports and teachers.

Encyclopedia and Charlie were the first to retire to the tent. They did what they had to do.

They stuffed their ears with cotton.

Nonetheless, Benny's snorts, whistles, and cackles woke Encyclopedia several times during the night. Benny's cry of dismay woke him at dawn.

"My wallet! It's gone!" Benny wailed. "I had ten dollars and my library card in it!"

Encyclopedia and Charlie helped Benny search the tent. Todd and Garth sat and watched.

"It isn't here." Benny groaned.

"Oh, yes, it is," Todd said. "Right, Charlie?"

"What do you mean?" Charlie demanded.

"I'll show you," Todd answered.

He went to Charlie's knapsack and pulled out a black wallet. "Is this yours, Benny?"

Benny gasped, "Y-yes," as Charlie stared in disbelief.

"Benny's snoring woke me about an hour ago," Todd stated. "The wallet was behind him on his air mattress. I guess it fell out of his back pocket while he was sleeping."

Encyclopedia raised an eyebrow.

"Charlie didn't know I was awake," Todd went on. "He was sitting up, rubbing his ears. He saw the wallet and hid it in his knapsack."

Encyclopedia gazed at the number 12 on the front and back of Benny's Detroit Lions shirt.

"If the wallet was behind Benny," the detective said to Todd, "then he lay snoring with his back to you?"

Todd grinned. "That's right."

"That's wrong," the detective said. "You stole the wallet and tried to frame Charlie."

How Did Encyclopedia Know?

(Turn to page 69 for the solution to
The Case of the Stolen Wallet.)

The Case of
the Manhole Cover

Lizzie Downing dashed into the Brown Detective Agency.

"I'm about to be rich!" she cried.

"You've got to have money to be rich," Sally pointed out.

"I'll have plenty," Lizzie insisted. "Wilford Wiggins said us little kids will soon be rolling in the stuff."

"Oh, brother." Encyclopedia moaned. "Wilford's up to his old tricks."

Wilford Wiggins was a high school dropout and too lazy to yawn. He lay in bed all morning thinking up ways to cheat little kids out of their savings.

Wilford never succeeded, however. Encyclopedia was there to shoot down his phony deals.

Only last week the detective had stopped Wilford from selling shares in an electric pillow that cured dandruff and increased brainpower while you slept.

"Wilford's called a secret meeting at the city dump for five o'clock today," Lizzie said. "It's by invitation only."

"We didn't get an invitation," Sally observed.

"Wilford doesn't like you two a whole lot," Lizzie replied. "Encyclopedia always sees through his sales pitches."

"Wilford's sales pitches always turn out to have a curve," Sally said.

"This time will be different," Lizzie declared. "I know it. Wilford swore he's gone straight."

As straight, Encyclopedia thought, *as a shepherd's staff.*

"Even the wool Wilford pulls over your eyes is half nylon," Sally said. "What's he selling today?"

"I'll find out at the secret meeting," Lizzie answered.

Suddenly she looked uncertain.

"Maybe I'd better hire you to come with me," she said. She laid a quarter on the gas can beside Encyclopedia. "I don't want to lose my savings."

Sally glanced at her watch. "It's ten minutes to five. We'd better hurry if we're going to catch Wilford's newest get-rich-quick idea."

"Before anyone gets poor quick," added Encyclopedia.

They reached the city dump as Wilford waved the crowd of small children closer.

"Gather round, gather round," he chanted.

The children moved in eagerly. They didn't want to miss one money-making word.

The smile smeared across Wilford's face suddenly disappeared. He had seen the detectives.

"I'm glad certain people are here, even if they weren't

invited to this secret meeting," he said smoothly. "Come as doubters, I say. Depart believing in Wilford Wiggins, your dollars' best friend."

"Aw, quit pumping the hot air," a girl shouted. "Get to the big money talk."

Wilford chuckled. He pointed to a square slab of metal by his right foot. "You know what this is?"

The children stared in puzzled silence.

"It's a manhole cover," Wilford crowed.

"Manhole covers are round," a boy hollered.

"Up until now," Wilford corrected. "What you're seeing is history in the making."

He tapped the handle folded into a niche cut in the surface of the manhole cover.

"With this handle a workman doesn't need a crowbar," Wilford sang. "He just lifts the manhole cover by the handle and climbs down into the sewer."

Wilford eyed his audience shrewdly.

"How come it's square?" he called. "More than a thousand round manhole covers were stolen last year in this country alone. Why? Because they're easy to roll away!"

Wilford tried to roll the square manhole cover and failed.

"There, you saw for yourselves!" he cried. "It's practically theft-proof. Besides, squares ones are cheaper to ship. You don't have to build special round crates. And you can stack them on edge in a truck. They won't roll around."

The children chattered among themselves. A square manhole cover made sense.

"Who but yours truly could have invented a square

manhole cover?" Wilford exclaimed. "I'm going to sell them to every city in the United States and elsewhere. Thousands of them! Millions!"

"Where do we come in?" a girl demanded.

"To be honest, I need to raise money to build a factory," Wilford confessed. "I'm willing to let my young pals in on this chance of a lifetime."

He paused for effect.

"I'm raising money by selling shares in my company," he continued. "You can buy as many as you like at five dollars a share."

Suddenly Wilford's eyes grew glassy, and he quivered like jelly. He seemed to have stunned himself.

"A mere five dollars a share?" he wailed. "My ears can hardly believe what my lips are saying. But I said it, and I'm a man of my word. Five dollars it is!"

The crowd of children hesitated, torn between doubt and greed.

"In two years," Wilford sang, "you'll be rich enough to put your mom and dad on an allowance."

That did it. The children began lining up to buy shares, cash in fist—until Encyclopedia stepped forward.

"Put your money away," he called, "if you don't want it to go down the sewer!"

What Does Encyclopedia Know?

(Turn to page 70 for the solution to
The Case of the Manhole Cover.)

The Case of the Two Spies

While biking to Jo-Jo's Ice Cream Shop, Encyclopedia noticed a man in a red shirt. Not far behind him was a man in a gray suit.

"The man in the gray suit was following the man in the red shirt, Dad," Encyclopedia said that night at dinner. "He followed him to a run-down hotel."

"The Martin Inn," Chief Brown said.

"Gosh, yes," Encyclopedia said. "How did you know?"

"The man in the gray suit is Arthur Colp, an FBI agent," Chief Brown explained. "The other man is John Hudson."

"Why is he being followed?" Mrs. Brown asked.

"Hudson worked for two years at the defense plant over in Glenn City," Chief Brown replied. "Two weeks ago he simply quit. The company believes he was spying."

"What is John Hudson doing in Idaville?" Mrs. Brown said.

"A man named Otto Severin had moved into the Martin Inn a week before Hudson did," Chief Brown said. "Severin worked in Chicago as a mechanic. The FBI believes he is a spy, too, and Hudson reports to him."

"If Hudson and Severin are working together," Mrs. Brown said, "why didn't they meet in Chicago?"

"Too risky," Chief Brown replied. "The FBI has kept a tight watch on Severin for months, and he knows it."

"Hudson and Severin are together now," Mrs. Brown pointed out. "In the old hotel."

"So far the two haven't met or talked to each other," Chief Brown said. "When Severin took a room near Hudson's, the FBI asked me to help keep watch on both men."

"How do you check their mail and telephone calls?" Mrs. Brown inquired.

"Neither Hudson nor Severin receives mail," Chief Brown answered. "The hotel lobby has the only telephone, and they don't use it. Hudson goes out in the morning. Severin goes out in the afternoon. Each man spends the rest of the time in his room."

"Don't they ever go to the same places?" Encyclopedia asked.

"Only in the morning," Chief Brown said. "The hotel is so old, it has but a single bathroom on each floor. Every morning Hudson and Severin shower, one after the other. But they don't even meet in the hall."

"You suspect Hudson is passing information about the defense plant in the bathroom?" Mrs. Brown asked.

"It sounds crazy, but I think so," Chief Brown said.

"You should take Leroy to the hotel," Mrs. Brown said. "Leroy can figure out how they do it."

"Want to help, son?" Chief Brown inquired.

"I'd like to try, Dad," Encyclopedia said.

On the drive to the Martin Inn, Chief Brown remarked, "I forgot to tell you one thing. Both Severin and Hudson have photographic memories. They don't forget anything."

The Martin Inn was a three-story walk-up covered with peeling paint and years. It looked ready to fall over.

Father and son climbed to the top floor. Encyclopedia saw three rooms on each side of a center hall. At the end of the hall was a door marked Bathroom.

All the doors, except the bathroom door, had a peep-hole.

"Hudson has the center room on the right, Severin the center one on the left," Chief Brown whispered. "My men and two FBI agents are in the other four rooms."

Chief Brown knocked softly on room 303.

The door was opened by Arthur Colp, the FBI agent whom Encyclopedia had seen following Hudson that morning.

"Anything new?" Chief Brown inquired.

"Same old story," Mr. Colp said. "Hudson goes out in the morning. Severin goes out in the afternoon. They sure don't hide messages anywhere."

"You search the bathroom after Hudson leaves and before Severin goes in, I trust?" said Chief Brown.

"And after Severin leaves as well," Mr. Colp answered. "Nothing is hidden in the pipes or anywhere else."

"How about their rooms?" Chief Brown said.

"We search them whenever Hudson or Severin goes out, as you instructed," Mr. Colp said. "Nothing but the usual stuff—clothes, toilet articles, towels, a few books. That sort of thing."

Mr. Colp looked baffled and angry.

"They're laughing at us," he said. "They know they're being watched. Yet somehow they're passing information under our noses. Otherwise, their living in the same hotel doesn't make sense."

Chief Brown gestured for Encyclopedia to slip out and investigate the bathroom.

The bathroom door stood open. Encyclopedia went in and closed the door behind him.

The room had a window, a toilet, a sink, and a shower. Encyclopedia searched every inch of everything.

He spent a moment staring at the mirror above the sink. Then he closed his eyes and thought his hardest.

"Of course," he murmured, and returned to room 303.

"When you check the bathroom after Hudson takes his shower and before Severin takes his," Encyclopedia asked, "is the window open?"

"Yes," said Agent Colp.

"And does Hudson leave the bathroom door open when he goes back to his room?"

"Wide open."

"There is your answer," Encyclopedia said. "Hudson and Severin chose this hotel because it is so old, it has only one bathroom on each floor. Perfect! They can pass secrets without ever being seen together."

How Did the Spies Pass Secrets?

(Turn to page 71 for the solution to
The Case of the Two Spies.)

The Case of
the Violinist's Chair

Sunday afternoon Encyclopedia and Sally went to the Collectors' Show at the Convention Center.

They had just walked through the door when Fay Xanikis came leaping toward them as though she had a bellyful of butterflies.

"Encyclopedia, Sally!" she cried. "Am I glad you're here. I saw my chair. Taggart Smith stole it!"

"Go over that again, please?" Encyclopedia requested.

Fay gulped breath and explained. Last month she had found a wooden armchair on a neighborhood trash pile. With her father's help he had fixed it up and put it out on her front porch. The next morning it was gone.

"I didn't see it again until today," Fay told the detectives. "Taggart is trying to sell it!"

"We'll see about that," Sally said.

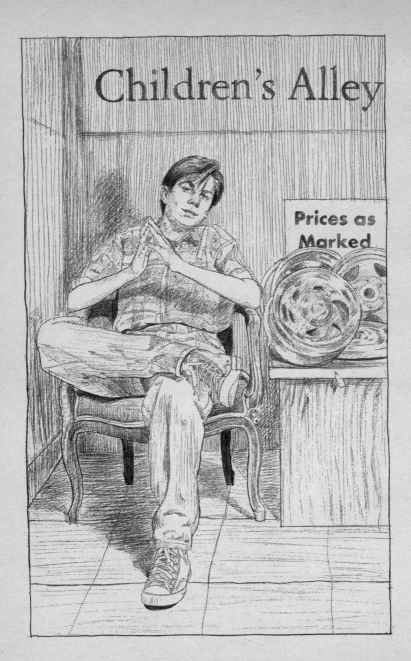

Encyclopedia didn't like Sally's tone, which she used when spoiling for a fight. He understood, however.

Taggart was the sixth-grade bully. His classmates rooted for the day he'd bring home a note from the principal demanding his absence.

"Where is the chair?" Sally asked.

"Taggart is sitting on it," Fay replied. "Follow me."

She led the detectives past tables piled with beer cans, old lunch boxes, doorknobs, quilts, and Transylvanian road maps.

"This show is for fun collectors," Fay said. "You won't see any fancy stuff like rare stamps or coins. And everything is for sale. You can pick up some real bargains."

She halted in a corner under a sign, **CHILDREN'S ALLEY**. Several little kids displayed their collections of trading cards, toys, bottle tops, marbles, and comic magazines.

Taggart Smith was sitting in a wood armchair. In front of him was a table loaded with hubcaps. A sign by his elbow read: **PRICES AS MARKED**.

Sally marched straight up to him. "Fay says the chair you're sitting on belongs to her."

Taggart bounded to his feet. "Her chair? Why, the kid needs oxygen."

"You stole it off my porch," Fay insisted.

"If you wish to buy it, I'll make you a special deal," Taggart purred. "The regular price is twelve dollars. But today only, I'll let it go for ten."

"I'm not buying back my own chair," Fay retorted. "I found it in a trash pile and fixed it up."

Taggart laughed. "I repaired this chair personally. I found it in the city dump."

"You couldn't find your head with both hands," Sally snapped.

"It's my chair and I can prove it," Fay said. "I scratched my initials, FX, under the seat."

Taggart didn't seem the least startled by the news. Indeed, he suggested having a look.

He turned over the chair. On the bottom of the seat was scratched FX.

"What did I tell you!" Fay exclaimed triumphantly.

Taggart smiled slyly. "Those aren't your initials, little girl. The FX stands for Francis Xanathippe."

Francis Xanathippe had been Idaville's finest musician. As a teenager he had started a business clipping and cleaning the hind half of cows. Farmers disliked the job, but a state law required it be done for sanitary reasons.

As he worked, Francis Xanathippe hummed to himself. Thus began his career in music. By the age of forty he was first violinist in the State Symphony Orchestra.

"This was the chair he sat in when he practiced at home," Taggart declared. "He died five weeks ago. Before his widow moved to Greece, she cleaned out the house. The old chair ended up in the dump."

"I never heard a worse lie!" Sally announced.

Taggart reddened. "That does it! I'm calling you out."

"After you," Sally said with a bow.

The detectives and Fay followed Taggart through a rear exit and into a narrow back alley.

Sally raised her fists. "Make your move."

Everything was happening so quickly. Encyclopedia had no chance to think about the chair. He could only watch and hope no one got hurt.

"One punch from me," Taggart snarled, "and you'll have tired blood for a month."

Sally wagged her right. "If I hit you with this, you'll be reading get-well cards tomorrow."

"Oh, yeah?" Taggart roared, and swung a haymaker. Sally slipped it and stung him with a rap on the ear.

Taggart stepped back, surprised.

He went into a dance, trying to confuse her with his speed. Sally was faster. Her jab beat "Taps" on his nose. Soon she had him wobbling around like a boy learning to walk on stilts.

"Curtain time," she said at last, and fired a fast one-two.

The two punches must have felt like ten. Taggart doubled over as if to get a closer look at the best place to land.

Fay hopped in glee. "Rest in pieces," she cried as Taggart sank to the ground.

He lay on his back, afraid to move. A girl had put him away. His bullying days were over.

Sally blew on her knuckles. Suddenly her brow knit in concern.

"Encyclopedia," she said, "you can prove he was lying about the chair belonging to Francis Xanathippe, can't you?"

Encyclopedia nodded pleasantly.

"Of course," he replied.

What Made Encyclopedia So Sure?

(Turn to page 72 for the solution to
The Case of the Violinist's Chair.)

The Case of
the Stolen Coin

"That was Officer Clancy on the phone just now," Chief Brown said. "Want to come along on a case, Leroy?"

"Do I!" Encyclopedia exclaimed. "What's it about, Dad?"

"A rare coin was stolen this evening from the home of two sisters, Betsy and Claire Millen," Chief Brown said. "We'll know more when we get there."

A ten-minute drive in the patrol car brought them to the Millen house on Meadowbrook Lane.

Officer Clancy was waiting at the curb.

"What have you got, Tim?" Chief Brown asked him.

"Just what I told you over the telephone, sir," Officer Clancy replied. "A nineteenth-century half dollar was stolen at the dinner table while the lights were out. The owner of the coin, Jay Cook, was unconscious. An ambulance was taking him away as I got here."

"Anyone else leave?"

"No," Officer Clancy replied, "and I'm told that nothing on the dinner table has been touched."

"Good," Chief Brown said. "Let's get started."

Two men and three women were in the dining room. Officer Clancy introduced them.

Encyclopedia studied the Millen sisters. Claire was broad shouldered and had a freshly scrubbed look. Betsy was slightly built and wore a great deal of makeup.

The others were Rodney Thomas, a pilot; Edgar Rice, a doctor; and Sara Lawson, an attorney.

"Will you all please take the same places you had at dinner?" Chief Brown requested.

The five took their seats at the round dining table. Betsy Millen and Dr. Rice sat on either side of the chair used by Jay Cook.

"Why did Jay Cook bring a valuable coin to the table?" Chief Brown inquired.

"We are a rare-coin club," Rodney Thomas explained. "We get together at a member's home once a month. At most meetings at least one of us shows a favorite coin."

"This evening Jay brought a half dollar," Sara Lawson said. "After it was passed around the table, Jay placed it by his water glass."

"Did anyone leave the table during the meal?" Chief Brown asked.

"I did, twice," Claire Millen said. "The first time I was in the kitchen carving the roast. The house went dark for about two minutes. A power failure, I suppose."

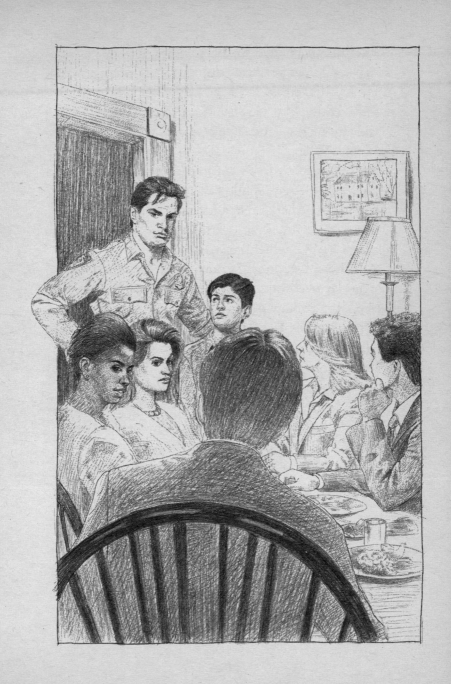

Chief Brown pointed to the empty water glass at Jay Cook's place. "Does he usually drink a lot of water?"

"Jay has diabetes," Dr. Rice said. "He has to drink water frequently."

"Did anyone leave the table besides you?" Chief Brown asked Claire Miller.

"No," she answered. "I went to the kitchen the second time to get the dessert. While I was there, the lights went off again but came back on in a few minutes."

"Before the lights went out the second time, did Mr. Cook seem sleepy?" Chief Brown asked.

"And how," Rodney Thomas said. "That's a joke among us. Jay overworks. He's always tired. Sometimes he falls asleep before dinner."

"When the lights came back on the second time," Chief Brown said, "was the coin still on the table?"

"It was gone," Betsy Millen said. "Officer Clancy searched all of us. None of us had it. When we couldn't wake Jay, I called the police."

"Jay was drugged, no question about it," said Dr. Rice. "But how? The drug wasn't in the food. The meal was passed around the table in serving dishes, and none of us was knocked out. Besides, it couldn't have been in the drinking water."

"Why not?" questioned Chief Brown.

"Because I forgot water glasses are set to the right of the plate," Dr. Rice said. "I drank from the glass on my left, Jay's glass. When I realized my mistake, I gave him my untouched glass."

"Don't forget the thin red line across the bridge of Jay's

nose," Sara Lawson put in. "It was there when the lights came on the second time."

"Oh, yes," Betsy Millen said. "I tried to bring Jay around with a cold wet cloth on his forehead. The red line wiped off."

"The strange part is that it looked like blood," Sara Lawson said. "Yet there was no bruise or cut."

Chief Brown asked to see the kitchen. Upon his return he motioned Encyclopedia into the hall.

"There are stairs from the kitchen to the basement," he said. "The way I see it, Claire Millen went from the kitchen down to the basement and threw a circuit breaker, cutting the electricity in the dining room. In the darkness her sister, Betsy, slipped knockout drops into Jay Cook's water glass."

"And after Claire put the lights back on," Encyclopedia said, "she waited for Mr. Cook to doze off. When he did, she went back to the kitchen to get the dessert—and to turn off the lights again."

Chief Brown nodded. "That gave Betsy Millen, who sat next to Cook, the chance to steal the half dollar."

"She had time to hide it before Officer Clancy arrived," Encyclopedia said. "Mr. Cook wasn't searched. So the thief can say Mr. Cook pocketed the coin when the lights went out, and it was stolen after he was taken to the hospital."

Chief Brown sighed heavily. "We need proof. The lab might tell us what kind of sleeping drug was slipped into Jay Cook's glass. But not who slipped it in."

"Did you notice that two other water glasses were empty?" Encyclopedia asked.

"Yes, Rodney Thomas's and Betsy Millen's."

"But only Betsy Millen's glass had lipstick on the rim," Encyclopedia said.

Chief Brown looked puzzled. "So?"

"So her glass is your proof, Dad!"

What Did Encyclopedia Mean?

**(Turn to page 73 for the solution to
The Case of the Stolen Coin.)**

Solutions

The Case of the Kidnapped Dog

The kidnapper, besides writing "on fifth of this month" instead of "Sunday," had written "at which" instead of "where," and "horn" instead of "telephone." Further, he had written "Mrs. Joan T." instead of "Mrs. Joan Todd," and "pooch" instead of "dog."

Encyclopedia realized the d and e keys on the kidnapper's computer keyboard were broken.

Chief Brown found a computer keyboard at a shop on South Street. The d and e keys were being repaired. The keyboard belonged to Mr. Gibson.

Mr. Gibson returned Royal Blackie in time for the Great Dane to win a first prize at the dog show.

The Case of the Fireflies

Encyclopedia talked Bugs into claiming he and his Tigers had caught the fireflies in the stadium.

But all the Tigers, working from nightfall to dawn in the stadium, could not have filled the can with fireflies.

Not in a week. Not in a month.

As Encyclopedia and Fanchon knew, the female firefly waits in bushes and tall grass for a mate to fly by.

In a stadium the female has no place to wait. There are no bushes, and the grass is cut short.

On a clear night only a few lost fireflies might be seen in a stadium, and probably none on a rainy night.

Bugs admitted he had lied and returned the fireflies to Fanchon.

The Case of the Duck Derby

Bugs wrote his name on the bicycle basket while the detectives were watching the races.

But his attempt to get revenge on Encyclopedia backfired.

To support his claim of theft he said he saw Encyclopedia bike into the park. He traced Encyclopedia's route to the tree by sweeping his arm from right to left.

True enough, but...

Anything moving from his right to his left would have shown him its left side.

Therefore Bugs couldn't have seen his name on the outside of the basket. He had written it on the right side.

The Case of the Sand Castle

Lance was guilty. He lied about not having been in the ocean that morning.

In truth, he had sneaked to and from Pablo's castle by the ocean. He knew the incoming tide would wash away his footprints.

He was afraid Pablo's castle would win, and so he had smashed it with a piece of driftwood before dawn.

However, Lance had forgotten that dogs love salt....

When Cuddles licked Lance's ankle, Encyclopedia realized that Lance had not taken a shower. The dog was licking the dried ocean salt on it.

When the judges heard from Encyclopedia, they awarded Lance's prize—a month's free ice cream at Jo-Jo's Ice Cream Shop—to Pablo.

The Case of the Telephone Call

Mr. Barton, Mrs. Miller, and Derek overlooked what "four-thirty" on the answering machine really meant.

They were upset and not thinking clearly.

The telephone order for the slippers came from Los Angeles, California. It was received in Atlanta, Georgia.

Los Angeles, California, is on the West Coast. Atlanta, Georgia, is in the East. The two cities are more than 2,000 miles apart and in different time zones.

Atlanta is three hours later.

When the caller in Los Angeles said it was four-thirty, it was seven-thirty in Atlanta. That was two and a half hours after Derek had left the office at five o'clock, Atlanta time.

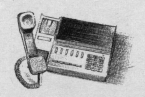

The Case of the Stolen Wallet

Todd and his brother, Garth, were mad at Charlie. He had made them throw back all their small fish. So Todd lifted Benny's wallet and tried to pin the theft on Charlie.

Todd had two problems with his story. First, he had to give a reason why both Charlie and he were awake late at night. So he blamed Benny's snoring.

Second, he had to explain how he could see the wallet. He couldn't have seen it if Benny was lying facing him, or on his back. So he claimed Benny had his back to him.

Only one of the statements could be true, Encyclopedia realized.

If Benny had his back to Todd, he was sleeping on his side. And when Benny slept on his side, "his snoring didn't bother a soul."

The Case of the Manhole Cover

Wilford fooled the small children with his square manhole cover.

He didn't fool Encyclopedia, however.

The detective knew the reason why manhole covers are always round. They cannot fall through the hole in the street.

A square manhole cover could fall if it were turned a certain way.

After the children had left the dump, Encyclopedia took a close look at Wilford's square manhole cover.

It was really the door to the furnace of an old French locomotive.

Wilford confessed. He had bought the door at a flea market for three dollars and sawed off the hinges.

The Case of the Two Spies

Hudson and Severin had photographic memories. So they didn't need to write anything down on paper.

Encyclopedia figured out why Hudson showered first. When the mirror was steamed, he wrote about the defense plant on it with his finger. Then he cleared the mirror by opening the window and leaving the door open.

Whenever one of the detectives slipped in, he saw a clear mirror.

Severin's shower caused the mirror to steam over again and show what Hudson had written! Severin then wiped the mirror clean.

Using a master key, Chief Brown surprised Hudson writing on the steam-coated mirror!

The Case of the Violinist's Chair

After stealing Fay Xanikis's armchair Taggart discovered her initials, FX, on it. He had to explain them.

The only other Idaville person he could think of with the initials FX was Francis Xanathippe. So Taggart said the chair had once belonged to Xanathippe.

But Taggart got carried away with his story. He claimed the violinist used the armchair when playing at home.

He thought no one could prove he lied. Xanathippe was dead. His widow had moved to Greece.

Taggart overlooked Encyclopedia's fast brain!

The detective knew that violinists sit in *armless* chairs while playing. Never in armchairs!

Caught in his lie, Taggart returned the chair to Fay.

The Case of the Stolen Coin

Chief Brown sent Jay Cook's water glass to the police lab. Encyclopedia had him send Betsy Millen's glass too. It was the only glass with lipstick on it.

Jay Cook's held no trace of a sleeping drug. Betsy Millen's glass did.

Encyclopedia knew she drugged her own glass, never dreaming it would be tested. She had switched glasses with Jay Cook when her sister put out the lights the first time.

In draining the glass dry, Jay Cook had tipped it till the rim touched his forehead. The lipstick on the rim left the "red line" between his eyes!

Betsy Millen then switched the glasses back before the lights went on again.

Jay Cook recovered. Although the sisters returned his coin, they were punished for drugging his water.